ADVENTURES WITH
Arnold Lobel

by Arnold Lobel

SMALL PIG

MOUSE TALES

UNCLE ELEPHANT

BARNES & NOBLE BOOKS

NEW YORK

This 2005 edition licensed for publication by Barnes & Noble Publishing, Inc.,
by arrangement with HarperCollins Publishers.

HarperCollins Publishers® and I Can Read Books® are registered trademarks.

ADVENTURES WITH ARNOLD LOBEL

Small Pig
Copyright © 1969 by Arnold Lobel

Mouse Tales
Copyright © 1972 by Arnold Lobel

Uncle Elephant
Copyright © 1981 by Arnold Lobel

Barnes and Noble Publishing, Inc.
122 Fifth Avenue
New York, NY 10011

ISBN: 0-7607-7107-3

Manufactured in China

05 06 07 08 09 MCH 10 9 8 7 6 5 4 3 2 1

SMALL
PIG

For Dreamnose

The small pig

lives in a pigpen on a farm.

The small pig likes to eat,

and he likes to run

around the barnyard,

and he likes to sleep.

But most of all

the small pig likes to sit down

and sink down

in good, soft mud.

The farmer and his wife
love the small pig.
"We think you are
the best pig in the world,"
they say.

One morning the farmer's wife says,

"Today I will clean my house."

She cleans the upstairs.

Then she cleans the downstairs.

"My house is spotless,"
says the farmer's wife,
"but the rest of this farm
is very dirty.
I will get to work
and clean it up."

The farmer's wife cleans the barn

and the stable

and the chicken coop.

15

Then she comes to the pigpen.

"Heavens!" cries the farmer's wife.

"This is the dirtiest spot of all."

16

So she cleans the pigpen,

and she washes the pig.

"That's better,"

says the farmer's wife.

"Now everything

is neat and shiny."

18

"Where is my good, soft mud?"
asks the small pig.
"I guess it is gone,"
says the farmer. "I'm sorry."

The small pig

is more than sorry.

He is angry.

"This place is too neat

and shiny for me," he says.

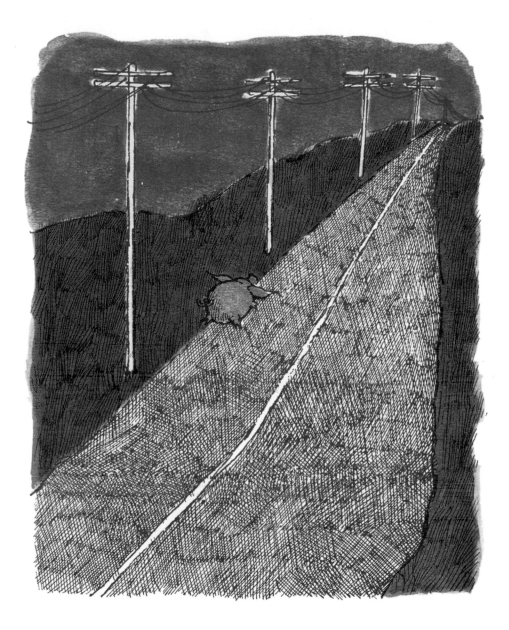

And that night

the small pig runs away.

Soon he finds a swamp.

"Ah!" cries the small pig.

"Here is good, soft mud."

The small pig sits down
and sinks down into the mud.
"Lovely, lovely," he says,
and then he goes to sleep.

"Ouch!" says the small pig

as a dragonfly bumps into his nose.

"Oops!" says the small pig

as a frog jumps onto his head.

"Yow!" says the small pig.

A turtle is biting his tail.

"Move yourself out of here!"

says a big snake.

"You are taking up space

that belongs to us."

26

So the small pig

moves himself out of there

in a hurry

and runs on down the road.

"Here is a very dirty place,"
says the small pig.

"There is sure to be
some good, soft mud nearby."

29

The small pig

finds broken bottles

and old television sets.

He finds kitchen sinks

and empty soup cans,

but he does not find mud.

"Cars are fun," says the small pig,

"but not as much fun as mud."

"Sofas are soft," says the small pig,

"but not as soft as mud."

Then he sees something

that he does not like at all.

"That is why there is no mud

around here!" cries the small pig.

And he runs on down the road.

At the end of the road

is a large city.

"Even the air is dirty here,"

says the small pig.

"There is sure to be

some good, soft mud nearby."

Soon the small pig

finds what he is looking for.

"Ah!" he says.

"Here is mud."

Then he sits down

and sinks down

into the good, soft mud.

"This mud is strange,"
says the small pig.
"It is not very soft at all.
In fact, it is getting harder
and harder."

He tries to get up,

but he cannot move.

Soon a few people

stop to stare

at the small pig.

40

More and more people

come to see

the small pig.

Then many, many people

come to look

because they have never seen

a pig stuck in the sidewalk.

45

The farmer and his wife

drive by in their car.

"Look at that big crowd

of people," says the farmer.

"Let's stop and see

what is happening."

"All right," says the farmer's wife,

"but hurry.

We must keep looking for

our lost pig."

The farmer stops the car.

"What is happening here?"

he asks a man.

"Oh, nothing much,"

says the man.

"There is just a pig

stuck in the sidewalk."

48

"Heavens!"

cries the farmer's wife.

"That is OUR pig

that's stuck in the sidewalk!"

"Call the police!

Call the firemen!"

shouts the farmer.

By this time
everyone
in the city
has come to see
the small pig.
The policemen
hold back
the huge crowd.

The firemen bring tools

to break the sidewalk.

52

"Please," says the farmer's wife,

"be very careful.

We think that pig

is the best

in the world."

The firemen work very carefully,

and soon

the small pig is free.

He jumps into the arms

of the farmer and his wife.

They all drive home together.

Just as they come to the farm

the sky turns dark,

and a storm begins.

It rains and rains.

59

The farmer says, "Look!
Now there is a brand new
mud puddle in the pigpen."
The farmer's wife says,
"And I promise
never to clean it up again."

60

So the small pig

runs into the pigpen.

First he has his supper.

Then he sits down

and sinks down

into the good, soft mud.

63

THE END

CONTENTS

THE WISHING WELL   8

CLOUDS   17

VERY TALL MOUSE
AND VERY SHORT MOUSE   25

THE MOUSE AND THE WINDS   32

THE JOURNEY   42

THE OLD MOUSE   48

THE BATH   55

"Papa, we are all

in bed now,"

said the mouse boys.

"Please tell us a tale."

"I will do better than that,"

said Papa.

"I will tell you seven tales—

one for each of you—

if you promise

to go right to sleep

when I am done."

"Oh yes, we will,"

said the boys.

And Papa began. . .

THE WISHING WELL

A mouse once found
a wishing well.
"Now all of my wishes
can come true!"
she cried.

She threw a penny

into the well

and made a wish.

"OUCH!"

said the wishing well.

The next day the mouse

came back to the well.

She threw a penny

into the well

and made a wish.

"OUCH!" said the well.

The next day

the mouse came back again.

She threw a penny

into the well.

"I wish this well

would not say ouch," she said.

"OUCH!" said the well.

"That hurts!"

"What shall I do?"

cried the mouse.

"My wishes

will never ever

come true this way!"

The mouse ran home.

She took the pillow

from her bed.

"This may help,"

said the mouse,

and she ran back

to the well.

The mouse threw the pillow

into the well.

Then she threw

a penny into the well

and made a wish.

"Ah. That feels

much better!"

said the well.

"Good!" said the mouse.

"Now I can start wishing."

After that day

the mouse made many wishes

by the well.

And every one of them

came true.

CLOUDS

A little mouse went for a walk
with his mother.
They went to the top of a hill
and looked at the sky.

"Look!" said Mother. "We can see
pictures in the clouds."

The little mouse and his mother
saw many pictures in the clouds.

They saw a castle...

a rabbit. . .

a mouse.

"I am going to pick flowers,"
said Mother.
"I will stay here
and watch the clouds,"
said the little mouse.

The little mouse

saw a big cloud in the sky.

It grew bigger and bigger.

The cloud became a cat.

The cat came nearer and nearer

to the little mouse.

"Help!" shouted the little mouse,

and he ran to his mother.

"There is a big cat in the sky!"

cried the little mouse.

"I am afraid!"

Mother looked up at the sky.

"Do not be afraid," she said.

"See, the cat has turned back

into a cloud again."

The little mouse

saw that this was true,

and he felt better.

He helped his mother pick flowers,

but he did not look up at the sky

for the rest of the afternoon.

VERY TALL MOUSE
AND VERY SHORT MOUSE

Once there was a very tall mouse
and a very short mouse
who were good friends.

When they met
Very Tall Mouse would say,
"Hello, Very Short Mouse."
And Very Short Mouse would say,
"Hello, Very Tall Mouse."

The two friends would often

take walks together.

As they walked along

Very Tall Mouse would say,

"Hello birds."

And Very Short Mouse would say,

"Hello bugs."

When they

passed by a garden

Very Tall Mouse would say,

"Hello flowers."

And Very Short Mouse

would say,

"Hello roots."

When they passed by a house

Very Tall Mouse would say,

"Hello roof."

And Very Short Mouse

would say,

"Hello cellar."

One day the two mice

were caught in a storm.

Very Tall Mouse said,

"Hello raindrops."

And Very Short Mouse said,

"Hello puddles."

They ran indoors to get dry.

"Hello ceiling,"

said Very Tall Mouse.

"Hello floor,"

said Very Short Mouse.

Soon the storm was over.

The two friends

ran to the window.

Very Tall Mouse held

Very Short Mouse up to see.

"Hello rainbow!"

they both said together.

THE MOUSE AND THE WINDS

A mouse went out in his boat,

but there was no wind.

The boat did not move.

"Wind!" shouted the mouse.

"Come down and blow my boat

across this lake!"

"Here I am," said the west wind.

The west wind blew and blew.

The mouse and the boat

went up in the air. . .

and landed

on the roof of a house.

"Wind!" shouted the mouse.

"Come down and blow my boat

off this house!"

"Here I am," said the east wind.

The east wind blew and blew.

The mouse and the boat

and the house

went up in the air. . .

and landed on the top of a tree.

"Wind!" shouted the mouse.

"Come down and blow my boat

off this house

and off this tree!"

"Here I am,"

said the south wind.

The south wind blew and blew.

The mouse and the boat

and the house and the tree

went up in the air. . .

and landed

on the top of a mountain.

"Wind!" shouted the mouse.

"Come down and blow my boat

off this house

and off this tree

and off this mountain!"

"Here I am," said the north wind.

The north wind blew and blew.

The mouse and the boat

and the house and the tree

and the mountain

went up in the air. . .

and came down into the lake.

The mountain sank
and became an island.

The tree landed on the island
and burst into bloom.

The house landed next to the tree.

A lady looked out of a window

in the house

and said,

"What a nice place to live!"

And the mouse just sailed away.

THE JOURNEY

There was a mouse

who wanted to visit

his mother.

So he bought a car

and started to drive

to his mother's house.

He drove and

drove and drove

until the car fell apart.

42

But at the side of the road

there was a person

selling roller skates.

So the mouse bought

two roller skates

and put them on.

He rolled and rolled

and rolled

until the wheels fell off.

But at the side of the road

there was a person

who was selling boots.

So the mouse bought

two boots and put them on.

He tramped and tramped

and tramped

until there were

big holes in the boots.

But at the side of the road

there was a person

who was selling sneakers.

So the mouse bought

two sneakers.

He put them on and ran

and ran   and ran

until the sneakers

were all worn out.

So he took the sneakers off

and walked   and

walked   and walked

until his feet hurt so much

that he could not go on.

But at the side of the road

there was a person

who was selling feet.

So the mouse took off his old feet

and put on new ones.

He ran the rest of the way

to his mother's house.

When he got there

his mother was glad to see him.

She hugged him  and

kissed him,

and she said, "Hello, my son.

You are looking fine—

and what nice new feet

you have!"

THE OLD MOUSE

There was an old mouse

who went for a walk every day.

The old mouse

did not like children.

When he saw them on the street

he would shout,

"Go away, horrid things!"

One day the old mouse
was taking his walk.
All at once, his suspenders broke,
and his pants fell down.

Some ladies came by.

"Help, help!" cried the old mouse.

But the ladies screamed,

"Your pants have fallen down!"

And they ran away.

The old mouse ran home

and cried, "Help me!"

But his wife only said,

"You look silly

in your underwear,"

and gave him a hit on the head.

The old mouse began to cry.

Some children passed by.

"Poor old mouse," they said,

"we will help you.

Here is some chewing gum.

It will hold your pants up

very well."

"Look!" cried the old mouse.

"My pants are up!

This chewing gum is great.

These pants will never

fall down again!"

Those pants never did
fall down again.
And after that, the old mouse
was always kind to children
when he went for his walk.

THE BATH

There was once a mouse

who was dirty,

so he took a bath.

The water

filled up the bathtub.

But the mouse was still dirty,

so he let the water

run over onto the floor.

The water

filled up the bathroom.

But the mouse was still dirty,

so he let the water

run out of the window.

The water

filled up the street.

But the mouse was still dirty,

so he let the water
run into the house
next door.

The people
in the house next door
cried, "Turn off the water!
We have had
our bath today!"

But the mouse was still dirty,

so he let the water

run all over the whole town.

The people in the town cried,

"Turn off the water!

You are very clean now!"

The mouse said,

"Yes, you are right.

I am clean now."

So he turned off the water.

By then

the town was all wet.

But the mouse

did not care.

He rubbed himself

with a big towel

until he was very dry.

And then

he went right to sleep.

"Is anybody awake?"

asked Papa.

There was no answer.

Seven small mice

were snoring.

"Good night, my boys,"

said Papa,

"and sleep well.

I will see you all

in the morning."

The End

UNCLE
ELEPHANT

For Charlotte Zolotow

UNCLE
ELEPHANT

CONTENTS

Uncle Elephant Opens the Door   6

Uncle Elephant Counts the Poles   11

Uncle Elephant Lights a Lamp   19

Uncle Elephant Trumpets the Dawn   25

Uncle Elephant Feels the Creaks   32

Uncle Elephant Tells a Story   37

Uncle Elephant Wears His Clothes   45

Uncle Elephant Writes a Song   51

Uncle Elephant Closes the Door   58

Uncle Elephant Opens the Door

Mother and Father

went for a sail

in their boat.

I could not go with them.

I had a runny trunk

and a sore throat.

I went home to bed.

There was a storm.

The boat did not come back.

Mother and Father

were missing at sea.

I was alone.

I sat in my room

with the curtains closed.

I heard my door opening.

"Hello, I am your Uncle Elephant,"
said a voice.

I looked at Uncle Elephant.

"What are you staring at?"
he asked.

"Ah, I know,
you are looking at my wrinkles."

"You *do* have many wrinkles,"
I said.

"Yes," said Uncle Elephant,

"I have more wrinkles
than a tree has leaves.

I have more wrinkles

than a beach has sand.

I have more wrinkles

than the sky has stars."

9

"Why do you have

so many wrinkles?" I asked.

"Because I am old,"

said Uncle Elephant.

"Now come out

of this dark place."

"Where will I go?" I asked.

"Come and visit me,"

said Uncle Elephant.

Uncle Elephant Counts the Poles

I sat

with Uncle Elephant

on the train.

We shared

a bag of peanuts.

We looked

out of the window.

11

The country

rushed past.

"One, two, three.

Oh, I missed one,"

said Uncle Elephant.

"What are you counting?"

I asked.

"I am trying to count

the houses

as they go by," he said.

"One, two, three, four.

I missed one again,"

said Uncle Elephant.

"What are you counting?"

I asked.

13

"I am trying to count
the fields
as they go by,"
he said.

"One, two, three, four, five.

I missed another one,"

said Uncle Elephant.

"What are you counting now?"

I asked.

"I am trying to count

the telephone poles

as they go by.

But everything is passing

too darn fast,"

said Uncle Elephant.

Uncle Elephant was right.

Everything *was* passing very fast.

15

"One, two, three,

four, five,

six, seven, eight,

nine, and ten!"

said Uncle Elephant.

"What are you counting

this time?"

I asked.

"I am counting

the peanut shells,"

said Uncle Elephant.

"They are easier to count.

They are all

in one place.

They are all

sitting on your lap."

17

The train raced along.

We finished

the whole bag of peanuts.

There were

many more shells

for Uncle Elephant

to count.

Uncle Elephant Lights a Lamp

We came to

Uncle Elephant's house.

"We will light a lamp

and have some supper,"

said Uncle Elephant.

He took a lamp

from the shelf and lit it.

19

"Hey there!"

said a small voice

from inside the lamp.

"Did you hear that?"

asked Uncle Elephant.

"This lamp can talk!"

"It is a magic lamp!" I said.

"Then we can make wishes!"

said Uncle Elephant.

"I wish for an airplane

that I can fly myself,"

I said.

"I wish for a polka-dot suit

with striped pants,"

said Uncle Elephant.

"I wish for a banana split

with ten scoops

of ice cream," I said.

"I wish for a box filled

with one hundred big cigars,"

said Uncle Elephant.

We rubbed the lamp.

We sat and waited.

A little spider

crawled out.

"I wish

that you would

turn off this lamp

and leave me

in peace,"

said the spider.

"I live in there.

It is getting hot."

Uncle Elephant made

the spider's wish

come true.

He was happy

to turn off the lamp.

Uncle Elephant

put the lamp

back on the shelf.

We ate our supper

by the light

of the moon.

Uncle Elephant Trumpets the Dawn

"VOOMAROOOM!"

It was morning.

I heard

a noise outside.

I ran to the window.

Uncle Elephant

was standing in the garden.

25

His ears flapped

in the breeze.

He raised his trunk.

"VOOMAROOOM!"

trumpeted Uncle Elephant.

"What are you doing?"

I asked.

26

"I always

welcome the dawn this way,"

said Uncle Elephant.

"Every new day

deserves a good,

loud trumpet."

27

"I have planted

all these flowers myself.

Come outside

and let me introduce you

to everyone,"

said Uncle Elephant.

"Roses, daisies,

daffodils and marigolds,

I want you

to meet my nephew."

I bowed to the flowers.

Uncle Elephant

was pleased.

"This garden

is my favorite place

in the world,"

said Uncle Elephant.

"It is

my own kingdom."

29

"If this is your kingdom,"

I said,

"are you the king?"

"I suppose I am,"

said Uncle Elephant.

"If you are the king,"

I said,

"I must be the prince."

"Of course,"

said Uncle Elephant,

"you *must* be the prince!"

We made ourselves

crowns of flowers.

Uncle Elephant raised his trunk.

"VOOMAROOOM!"

I raised my trunk.

"VOOMAROOOM!"

We were the king

and the prince.

We were trumpeting the dawn.

Uncle Elephant Feels the Creaks

Uncle Elephant

and I

went for a walk.

"Ouch!"

cried Uncle Elephant.

"What is the matter?"

I asked.

"I am feeling the creaks,"

said Uncle Elephant.

"What are the creaks?"

I asked.

"Sometimes they happen

to old elephants like me,"

he said.

"My back creaks,

my knees creak,

my feet creak,

even my trunk creaks.

The creaks

are quite uncomfortable."

We walked slowly home.

Uncle Elephant

sat down carefully

in his softest chair.

"Ah," he said,

"the creaks in the bottom

part of me are gone."

Uncle Elephant

rested his head

on the back of the chair.

"Ah," he said,

"the creaks in the top

part of me are gone."

Uncle Elephant

put his legs on a footstool.

"Ah," he said.

"The creaks in my feet

are gone."

"Are you feeling better?"

I asked.

"Almost,"

said Uncle Elephant.

"If you let me

tell you a story,

I am sure all of my creaks

will go away."

Uncle Elephant Tells a Story

"Once there was

a King and a Prince,"

said Uncle Elephant.

"The Prince was brave.

He was young and smart.

The King was old.

He had many wrinkles.

"They lived in a castle

at the edge of a woods.

One day the King

and the Prince

went for a walk.

They became lost

in the woods.

'Oh, help!'

cried the King.

'Do not worry,'

said the Prince.

'We will

find our way home.'

" 'Oh, help and ouch!'

cried the King.

'I am tired.

I am creaking all over.

I want to go home.

I want to sit in my chair.'

"They wandered

in circles for hours.

They could not

find their castle.

A lion jumped out at them.

'A king and a prince!

Just what I want for dinner!'

roared the lion.

"He showed them his sharp teeth.

The King and the Prince

raised their trunks.

'VOOMAROOOM!'

They both trumpeted

as loudly as they could.

The lion was so afraid

that every one of his teeth

popped out.

He ran away.

"The King tried to look

over the tops of the trees.

'My old eyes are weak,'

he said.

'I can't see a darn thing.'

'King,' said the Prince,

'my eyes are sharp.

Lift me up on your head.'

The King lifted the Prince.

"The Prince looked

over the tops of the trees.

'There it is!' he cried.

'I can see the tower

of our castle.

Now we are not lost!'

"And that," said Uncle Elephant,

"was how the King and the Prince

helped each other

to find their way home."

Uncle Elephant had ended his story.

"There," he said, "that does it.

From top to bottom

I do not feel a single creak!"

Uncle Elephant Wears His Clothes

There was a picture

in Uncle Elephant's

living room.

"That is a picture of me

when I was your age,"

said Uncle Elephant.

I looked at the picture.

45

Uncle Elephant

was with

his mother and father.

They looked

just like mine.

I felt sad.

I began to cry.

Uncle Elephant looked sad too.

"Now, now," he said,

"let's not have

any of this.

I must do something

to make us happy.

46

"I will wear

some funny clothes.

That will make us smile."

Uncle Elephant

opened his closet door.

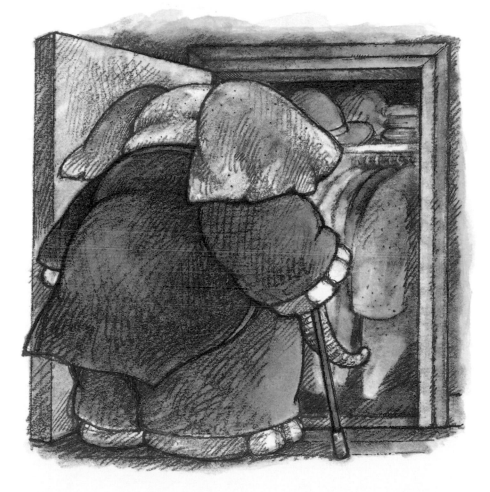

He looked at his hats

and his ties and his shirts

and his pants and his jackets.

"My clothes are not funny,"

said Uncle Elephant.

"What can I do?"

Uncle Elephant

went into his closet.

In a while he came out.

He was wearing

all of his hats, all of his ties,

all of his shirts, all of his pants,

and all of his jackets.

Uncle Elephant

was wearing everything

on top of everything.

Uncle Elephant

was a pile of clothes

with two big ears.

First I smiled.

Then I giggled.

Then I laughed.

We both laughed so hard,

we forgot to feel sad.

Uncle Elephant Writes a Song

"Sing a song for me,"

said Uncle Elephant.

"I don't know any songs,"

I said.

"Not one?"

asked Uncle Elephant.

"Not even one," I said.

"Then I will write you
a song of your own,"
said Uncle Elephant.
He wrote the words
of the song
on a piece of paper.

"I have a song.

It's an elephant song.

I will sing it

whenever I please.

With my trunk in a loop,

I will sing while I swoop

from the vines

and the branches of trees.

53

"I have a song.

It's an elephant song.

I will sing it

wherever I go.

Upside down on my head,

with my ears as a sled,

I will sing

as I slide through the snow.

54

"I have a song.

It's an elephant song.

I will sing it

whatever I do.

When I sing while I munch

on my peanutty lunch,

I will not miss a note

as I chew.

55

"I have a song.

It's an elephant song.

I will sing it

and never forget

that, of all music played,

there is no better made

than an uncle

and nephew duet."

56

Uncle Elephant

made up a tune

to go with

the words.

Together, we sang

my song.

We sang it

over and over.

57

Uncle Elephant Closes the Door

One day a telegram came

to Uncle Elephant's house.

It was from

my mother and father!

They had been

found and rescued.

They were alive!

Uncle Elephant

and I

danced for joy.

"I must take you home

at once," he said.

I sat

with Uncle Elephant

on the train.

We looked

out of the window.

"One, two, three, four..."

said Uncle Elephant.

"Are you counting the houses?"

I asked.

"No," said Uncle Elephant.

"Are you counting the fields?"

I asked.

"No," said Uncle Elephant.

"I know," I said.

"You are counting

the telephone poles."

"No,"

said Uncle Elephant.

"Not this time."

61

Mother and Father

were waiting for us.

I rushed into their arms.

That night,

after a fine dinner,

I sang my song.

Uncle Elephant

played the piano.

62

Before I fell asleep,

Uncle Elephant came into my room.

"Do you want to know what I was

counting on the train?" he asked.

"Yes," I said.

"I was counting days,"

said Uncle Elephant.

"The days we spent together?"

I asked.

"Yes," said Uncle Elephant.

"They were wonderful days.

They all passed too fast."

We promised

to see each other often.

Uncle Elephant

kissed me

good night

and closed

the door.